**Amber Tamblyn** is a contributing writer for the Poetry Foundation and the author of two previous works of poetry, *Free Stallion* and *Bang Ditto*. As an actress, she has been nominated for an Emmy, a Golden Globe, and an Independent Spirit award. Her writing has appeared in *Bust*, *Interview*, *Cosmopolitan*, the *San Francisco Chronicle*, *Poets & Writers*, *Pank*, and elsewhere. She lives in Los Angeles, California, and Brooklyn, New York.

## Also by Amber Tamblyn

*Bang Ditto*

*Free Stallion: Poems*

# Dark Sparkler

## Amber Tamblyn

HARPER ● PERENNIAL

NEW YORK ● LONDON ● TORONTO ● SYDNEY ● NEW DELHI ● AUCKLAND

HARPER  PERENNIAL

HarperCollins books may be purchased for educational, business, or sales promotional use. For information, please e-mail the Special Markets Department at SPsales@harpercollins.com.

*Designed by Leah Carlson-Stanisic*

*Cover art image of face and used on pages iii, 39, 43, 75, 75, and 94-95 © CSA Images/ Archive/Getty Images*

*Author photo credit: Photo by Katie Jacobs*

Poems in *Dark Sparkler* have appeared in the following places: "Brittany Murphy": *Pank* Magazine. "Miriam Lebelle": *The Nervous Breakdown.* "Bridgette Andersen," "Shannon Michelle Wilsey," and "Aubrey May" in *H_NGM_N.* "Bridgette Andersen" also appeared in *Chorus: A Literary Mixtape*, edited by Saul Williams (MTV Books). "Laurel Gene": *Thrush* and the *Iowa Review.* "Li Tobler," "Taruni Sachved," and "Marilyn Monroe" (as "Norma Jean Mortenson"): *Tuesday Journal.* "Miranda Rose," with its Sage Vaughn art, and "Miriam Labelle" and Jane Doe," with their Pat Hamou art, in *Black Tongue Review.* "Sirkka Sari," "Carole Landis," and "Anissa Jones" in *Forklift Ohio.* "Judith Barsi" and "Peg Entwistle" in the *Iowa Review.* "Sharon Tate," "Dana Plato," and "Marilyn Monroe" (as "Norma Jean Mortenson") in *The Rattling Wall.* "Quentin Dean" and "Untitled Actress" in the *Pacific Coast Poetry Series Anthology.* A portion of "Epilogue" in the Academy of American Poets' Poem-a-Day series at http:// www.poets.org/poetsorg/poem-day.

Library of Congress Cataloging-in-Publication Data has been applied for.

ISBN 978-0-06-234816-6

15  16  17  18  19  OV/QGT  10  9  8  7  6  5  4  3  2  1

for my father, the author Russ Tamblyn

# Contents

# Foreword

Warning: the book you are holding in your hands will break your heart.

Not a word of *Dark Sparkler* is "poetic" in the foolish and flowery sense. None of it is symbolic. Amber Tamblyn is not playing with metaphor or some flight of fancy. She is gifting us with the tragedy, the power, and most of all the *truth* of these women's lives.

*Dark Sparkler* is many things. It is, first of all, wonderful poetry. It is also cartography in that it maps a previously unexplored piece of women's experience—a part of the map with which Ms. Tamblyn is personally familiar.

It is also a memorial and a magical act. Because it is all these things, I thought to suggest a way *in*:

First, read *Dark Sparkler* as you would any new poetry book that comes into your hands. Open it at random and read here and there (if that's your way), or "begin at the beginning" like Alice, go on till you reach the end, then stop. Look at the pictures. *Enjoy.*

At some point you will begin to get curious. Something will start to tug at the edge of your mind/heart. At that point, go to the library or search the Internet for information about any girl/woman you find yourself thinking about. Look up Peg Entwistle, Bridgette Andersen, Samantha Smith. Read their (often sadly short) stories. Let your imagination fill in what book and computer don't say.

If you get addicted to these poems, as I did, you may find that you begin to print out certain bios and/or pictures—photos, sketches, even daguerreotypes. You will have made your own "companion volume," one you can turn to when you reread *Dark Sparkler*. Which you will probably do again and again.

—*Diane di Prima*

# Dark Sparkler

# Li Tobler

When you find a skull in the woods,
do you leave it alone because it disturbs you
or do you leave it alone
because of what's still living

inside?

# Untitled Actress

Submission calls for an actress mid-to-late 20s. All ethnicities acceptable. Except Asian-American. Caucasian preferable. Must read teen on-screen. Thin but not gaunt. Lean. Quirky but not unattractive. No brown eyes. Not taller than 5'5". Weight no more than 109. Actress should have great smile. Straight teeth a must. Must be flexible. Small bust a plus. Can do own stunts. Will waive rights to image, likeness, publicity, and final cut.

Role calls for nudity. Role calls for simulated sexual intercourse. Role calls for role play with lead male. No stand-in avail. Role pays scale.

Character is shy yet codependent, searching for love in all the wrong men. Character confides in others at her own risk. Character is fatigued and hollow, suffers from self-doubt, a sense of worthlessness. Character learns the hard way to believe in herself. No brown eyes. Character finally finds happiness when she meets Brad, a successful older businessman, 5'5".

Log line: A woman fights to save her soul. Think a young Carole Lombard meets a younger Anna Nicole. Requires an actress that will leave an audience speechless, who's found her creative voice.

Not a speaking role.

# Thelma Todd

This Svedka-sponsored T-Mobile party
tucked into the tight shoulder blades of the Pacific Palisades
is honoring the lifetime achievements of Christina Aguilera.

In the background Debbie Harry croons
for a terrace of people titillated for the songs
of incoming messages.
I'm in some charcoal hallway, cornered
by an actress in a bandage dress,
burned one too many times,
whose cocktail is doing all the healing,

sloshing on about the good ol' days,
back when we were all periodless and vivacious,
our winning auditions clinging to our underwear.

How we'd piss victory,
brush the rejection from our hair.

She wants to know what I think of Annie—
how vulgar her success is,
what a tragedy it's all become,
am I also allergic to her over-enunciations?

She wants to know if I've heard
about the role opposite the handsome future failure,
am I getting in line
to lose weight for the seventh-chance director.

Do I want advice, in general, but more specifically,
on how to blow up my breasts
into fame balloons,

send them up to the helium angels
on a string body?

*Your career has another five years, maybe,* she says, *if you're lucky.*
*According to who?* I ask.
*According to every actress who's come before you.*

So I turn my focus to every actress
coming after me.

I wade through the crowd with a canister of judgment,
tag the train of every dress, leave my mark
on their scars.

At the bar I run into Nancy,
drinking away her forties,
her eyes are flush broken compasses.
Lost between age fifteen and fifty.

Fermented blood.
Deep-sea drinker.

I do not look into her ocean.
The fish there float to the bottom.
I fear I'll go down there too,
identifying with the abyss.
Washed up.
Banging on the back door of a black hole.

I plow through the women's room doors
into cool tiled silence.
Run warm water over my shaking hands.
Above the sink, above the mirror,
a picture of the bar's first owner stares down at me,

that Dust Bowl—era actress
who killed herself in that Lincoln
or fell asleep with the engine running.
Maybe it was a Packard convertible.

She would've had to make her comeback too.

When the coroner cut her open, he found only
peas and beans in her stomach. No blue moonstones
beneath old-fashioned bandages.

I look down at the sink, the water brimming over
the tops of my wrists and onto the floor.
I do not tell my fingers what to do.
My hands are not my hands. They are the water
surrounded by swirling, singing, overflowing stars.

# Miriam Lebelle

I'm told Joni Mitchell took my newborn baby feet into her palms,
called them sweet cashews and kissed their soles.
I lay there in my father's arms, a sedated frog,
a fleshy spit of fresh molecule juice.

I'm told women have more nerve endings in their hands than men.
That this is a scientific fact.

I'm told Galileo wept at how big his hands looked,
how small they felt,
while pointing at the stars.

A book written by every one of God's representatives tells me
Salvation is for everyone except God.

I'm told your poems are about me. All of them.
Even when they're about "Jennifer."
Even when dedicated to "mother."

I was told we met in the nineties. You shook my hand and told me
I would not remember you saying that I am the love of your life.

I'm told in thirty-eight years I will lose a child.
The psychic on Astor Place charges me only ten dollars.

I'm told we should write more vague prayers for rock stars
and send them up into the sky on helium balloon strings.

She was told you kept her letters like Bazooka gum wrappers.
You broke her cigarette heart like an addict who wanted saving.

But the only thing you know how to love, I'm told,
is the sound of cheap plastic high heels on pavement.
The click-clack of flim-flam.

I'm told there's a balcony
where my old dresses are hung to dry in Detroit.

I'm told they buried the body with the garter belt still on.

# Judith Barsi

Plucked:
All the cat's whiskers
girl's eyebrows
eyelashes
cactus thorn
cored heart
dialogue from the page
cattle call
fish from the feeding tube
star sticker stuck on the star fucked over
pool bottom baby tooth
last exhale
gasoline receipt under driver's seat
bullet pulled from box springs
mattress grows scorpion legs in aunt's dreams
scalp on the stucco
story line
arc
conclusion
glass animals from the cinder
initials in sidewalk concrete
the shadows of initials
at dawn
in the cemetery

# Peg Entwistle

Her Jetticks could always be seen in the dark, even as she climbed into the cold blackened breastbone of the Hollywood Hills. It's why she loved them so much: Her shoes. Their demand for existence, their inability to disappear. Their worn-in seams had carried her body over the years, over America's canyons, over various important thresholds. They had been wrenched off by the thumbs of impatient lovers and drenched in the ilk of the Pacific Ocean's ornaments. They had always known where she was going long before she did.

*Let's go off the road this time,* they whispered up to her.

*Let's reenact the childhood of Virginia Woolf, collect only the moths attracted to black. Look how sturdy on raw granite we still are? We'll fight the yellow star thistles and wear them as spurs. We'll keep the gopher snakes away from your pleats and kick you up the scents of sagebrush and night-blooming jasmine. Tonight, you are endemic to Hollywood.*

She could always count on them. Their faded color could still ruffle up a reflection of the candlelight from the new moon's dinner parties. Their inch-high heels sowed the Griffith Park ground, a trail of bread crumbs for the seeds of Spanish moss arriving on old wind.

*When you get to the top, Peg, take us off, climb up that letter's ladder. Tell us what you see.*

She put her bare feet on the land.
It was the spine of an ancient dragon's carcass, one she'd slain lifetimes ago.

She climbed the white H in the HOLLYWOODLAND sign,
occasionally looking down at the black clouds of chaparral floating on
the earth.

*We can see up your dress!* her Jetticks teased. *Nice hosiery, ma cherie!*

*Shhhhh!* she teased back. *Everyone knows all the coyotes are drag queens
in Los Angeles! They will come and try to wear you if you're not quiet!*

The wind began to move in an unfamiliar way.
Her senses shifted like water striders over ripples.
The ground felt incidental.

For the first time, she shifted her gaze down
at her bare feet, naked and crooked.
Wild and full of sudden language.
She knew they had carried all the secrets of her shoes.
What did they know?

She wanted to know
what it'd be like to get seen in the dark.
To make the first move.

She looked up and out and jumped
into the stars, into the famous
valley of light.

# Jean Harlow

In black and white
the shadows of her eyelashes
like famous film nuns falling on ivory saints
black and white
her illnesses were not
black and white
kidneys couldn't even agree on a shade
black and white
she was so pale
someone needed to balance her out
with black
And white? The chipped tooth of a czar
a scar on the sun
look how she squints
her lover blinds her
something black and white
she smiles like the opening of a piano lid
with no black and whites
she rolled the dice of a career and saw no
numbers just black and white
what a depression-era star knows is
no blacks just whites
with a mole so black
and hair so white
she told the doctor she feared the dark
that it felt like she was looking into the light
there there they all told her

and made her sign away her
black on the white

And the beginning of Technicolor
meant the end of

but blood dried on the hospital sheets
will always be

# Martha Anne Dae

And I remember you chasing butterflies with a pasta strainer,
screaming, *Drop your antennae! Put up your weapons!*
Your face an arsonist's painting,
your cheeks freckled in the ash of pubescent rage.

You caught them, crushed their bodies with your fragile fingers
until it was your limbs that were winged,
your hands covered in mashed melanin pigments.

*See?* you said.
*They aren't the only ones who can fly.*

And I remember your stems, flying softly in no particular wind,
dusted in a young violence,
the strainer forgotten
as your body reached like a bow toward the sky,
and every last arrowhead was unearthed from your eyes.

How your arms carried you into silence
like a single creature falling
lifeless from a migration.

# Jayne:

Much love, your friend, George

# Jayne Mansfield

Your neck was a study of the asterisk,
the silken shape of Sanskrit,
the sucker punch of succulents.

Your neck a thinning glacier,
fine as the grind of a blade curve,

soft as a *k* in a known word
long as they say about slow burns.

Your neck the place where pearls retired
below the face your girls admired.

Your neck was a fortune you did not spend.
Your neck is what they'll remember the most.
Your neck in the end.

# Carole Landis

My heart's always been in the right place:
On all that's steel in a Fairfield February
Climbing up the fingers of the sun to sleep
in the deep slits of its wrists
Hula hooping my way into a new era's horse operas
Watching a pier burn into the blue bier of Santa Monica Bay
In the roots of a Polish farm girl's hair.

My heart will always be in the right place:
             In the caught talk of history's hingeless jaw
      You say Seducing Seconal
               I say Seconal the Seducer
         At the front line of my ending,
                 At the bottom of the mountain,
           looking down.

# Anissa Jones

My heart's always been in the right place:
In the worn levees of West Lafayette
Floating with the crocodile behind its hunter
In a jar of dead fireflies my brother left under the sun.

My heart will always be in the right place:
In the caught talk of history's hingeless jaw
You say Seducing Seconal
I say Seconal the Seducer
At the front line of my ending,
At the bottom of the mountain,
looking down.

# Susan Peters

My hands in your hair. My fingers down your chest. My feet in the
warm summer mud. My hips opening to a stand. You drinking the
coral from my elbows. Your hands casting spells under my dress.
Your fingers the magic wands. Your hips folding around my body like
a famous novel's sleeve. The taste of gin. Of salt, of mustard. Warm
celery left out on the picnic blanket, the taste of grapes, swallowing
wine, swallowing fog, swallowing you. The feel of bare ankles. Willow
brushing across my knees through a field. A silk hem. Stockings. Your
kisses rising like an elevator up my legs, each muscle a floor with an
appointment you've arrived early for. You take your time. Taker of
time. Your feet rubbing against mine under our sheets. *Our sheets.* My
feet standing on top of my father's when I was a child. This is how I
learned to dance. You wanting to waltz outside the Mayfair. You loving
my glide. You rubbing the skin of a peach on my Achilles. You licking
the bleak roe out from under my fingernails. My nipples explode in
your mouth like small brown cannons. The taste of meat. Of game. Of
duck. Even after what happened, of duck. Strawberries. Lime. Pickled
okra, soft butter, soft-boiled eggs in the morning, the smell of your
strong coffee and undercooked bacon. The smell of your cologne in
the other room. The feel of a blade through onion, blade through
fat, through fennel root, carrot, ginger, pecan pie. Blade in the jam,
blackberry on rye, sour cherry and sweet cheese on buckwheat. You
feeding me basil and sorrel from our garden. *Our garden.* Champagne
from our successes. *Our successes.* Fresh mint paste from France for
our toothbrushes. *Our toothbrushes.* My hands, dressing you, back
before you had to lean down so I could straighten your tie. Button
your collar. Lick a hair back into line with those other silver soldiers.
Kiss you good-bye, my hands in your hair, fingers down your chest.
You pulling me in. My lower back like your gloves. Your favorite

gloves by the front door where we kept the mail in our house. Our house. Our house. Our house. Our home. *Our.* The taste of orange. Of stomach acid. Iron. My tongue dark and thin as a stewed bay leaf. The taste of bittersweet. Of ash. Of my own medicine. Of resignation. Waterlessness. My hands in my own hair, my fingers on my chest. You gone. My body, cold winter mud getting colder.

# Dominique Dunne

First, he stood very still in her driveway,
waiting for her to come out.

No. First she stood in the living room
talking the silk off a sultan with her costar.
Then she heard a voice say, *Dominique, come outside please. Alone.*

But first, the telephone continued its kidnapping of air,
screaming like a car brake teething on a tire wheel.

No. First she screamed with laughter
as the costar made a hat out of a teacup.
Then she couldn't take the preaching landline anymore,
ripped the receiver off its soapbox.

But first, the costar arrived at her front door smiling,
a box of black licorice and a script under his arm.

No. First she got ready for the costar.
Then she heard something. Or maybe it was just her imagination.

But first, she took her grandfather's sheath into the shower,
tucked it under the soap.
Washed her hair as quietly as possible with the bathroom door open,
listening.

No, first she asked her father to install a dead bolt.
Then relief: that pile of dirty clothes behind her bed
was not a man crouched.

But first she said, *I'm sorry, Charles, it's over between us,*
tied together the sheets of their love letters,
climbed out the window of his soul.

No—first—he said—no, warned her—not to do this.
To make him show up at her house,
matchsticks crawling from his mouth,
fingers dripping like horns pulled from the fatal stab.

## Sirkka Sari

I pulled a caterpillar off its leaf in the hotel garden
and placed it in my rolling paper with the tobacco.
I could feel it squirm as my tongue ran across the edge, sealing it in.

I smoked it and thought of her.

I found the marrowless leg bone of a lynx.
I held up the white tube toward the sky
and stared at the sun through the hollow.

I did not blink and thought of her.

I collect eyelashes from the used pillows of guests
every time I clean a room.
I boil water and place all of them inside.
I pour their dreams and before I drink,
I blow.

I make a wish and think of her.

# Cindy Jenkins

The doctor hands me a piece of chalk,
asks me to draw an outline
illustrating how big I think I am. I draw
a door on the floor and tell him, *This is where dad
used to take me for dinner.*

## Brittany Murphy

Her body dies like a spider's.
In the shower,
the blooming flower
seeds a cemetery.

A pill lodges in the inner pocket of her flesh coat.
Her breasts were the gifts of ghosts.
Dark tarps of success.

Her mouth dribbles
onto the bathroom floor.
Pollock blood.

The body is lifted from the red carpet,
put in a black bag,
taken to the mother's screams
for identification.

The Country says good things
about the body.

They print the best photos;
the least bones, the most peach.

Candles are lit in the glint
of every glam. Every magazine stand
does the Southern belle curtsy
in her post-box-office-bomb honor.

The autopsy finds an easy answer.
They say good things about the body.

How bold her eyes were, bigger than Hepburn's.
The way she could turn in to her camera close-up
like life depended on her.

# Bridgette Andersen

A child-star actress is a double-edged dildo.
~~(Insert a metaphor about getting screwed here.)~~

No one should have to look back to see
the bright future ahead of them. The future holds

then pushes you away.
I'm gonna tie those pamphlets for cures
around this needle
and wave the white flag.

I just want to lean into the duct tape
this vial is holding up to my mouth.
Cut creativity's circulation off.
Get some rubber nooses together and gangbang my arm.

Growth has outgrown me.
I'd rather not be a word
associated with weeds and dicks.

I'd rather spend all that future brightness
looking up La Brea's sparkling skirt at dawn.

Hitchhiking up that boulevard's famous slit,
catching a ride with some opiates and trading spit.

I've heard Junk is starring in Scorsese's next movie.
This syringe knows people.

Forget my mother and father in all this.
They are a language that died on an ancient tongue.

I'm going to floss my teeth with the pubic hair

of the Hollywood night air,
memorize my lines before I snort them.

I want to know what it feels like
to die in the arms of missing limbs.

To end an act in my own skin,
covered in someone else's skeleton.

To get on my knees and crawl
on all fours into character.

To fade to black,
then fade through that.

# Shannon Michelle Wilsey

## A Poem for Bridgette Andersen
by Savannah

They call me Silver Kane
spelled with a *k* or with a *c*,
or sometimes it's just Silver plain,
I don't care long as they're calling me.

But I am Savannah mostly to this world and
I gave myself that name after you.
Like your character I'm a runaway girl,
giving in to men who want to protect me too.

I know just how it feels
to want nothing more than to be loved.
What we have in common gives us our appeal—
the fact we never got enough.

They say it looked like a big flower had sprung
in the place where I shot myself dead,
just like those ribbon pigtails clung
onto either side of your head.

# Jane Doe

Why do you insist on wearing
that sugarcoat
in the July of your life?

Why don't you feel more like a riot,
less like the cops?

I want to look you in the shards.

Go down on your cliché
until your taboo kabooms.

What's the point of sobriety
when you can *be* the cherry on top,
when you can put confetti in the condom,
pussy pop in clogs,
wrap yourself in Christmas lights.

What's the point of playing it safe
when you can make a tambourine
out of any two objects.

Wrestle the Ayn Rand impersonator
for her flask,
or better yet,
put the straw directly into the bottle,
avoid the apocalypse altogether?

What's the point of sweating the details
when I can just purchase the theremin
online?

So let's drop the socialization charade.

This life's too short
and the only way to extend it
is with a skirt that's too short.

A reminder for any man's hungry eyes
that I shit out of that.

I'm not interested in going out with a bang.
I'm interested in going out
with your father.

I want to teach you how to make origami
from a page by Frank O'Hara.
Fortune Fuck-Hundred.
Let's get undressed in each other's mouths.
Skinny dip lips.

I know what you're thinking and you're right.
That's just the revolution talking.

That's just the Sunday I'm gonna answer
your prayers with.

This is the film
I could finally get cast in.

# Heather O'Rourke

INT. HEATHER O'ROURKE'S HOSPITAL ROOM—NIGHT

Facing a window is our heroine, **HEATHER O'ROURKE** (12). Her sweaty blond hair capsizes over the sanitary pillow. Her closed eyes rest in dark halos on her face. Her hands lie small and creamed like new tulips. O.C. we hear the faint sound of white noise.

CUT TO:

The television, its volume low. O.C. behind the television, a door CLICKS OPEN. We pan to reveal a DARK FIGURE emerging into the room, out of focus. Heather doesn't move to look.

HEATHER
Is it time? I want to be with Dominique again.

We stay on Heather as O.C. we hear the click of the television being TURNED OFF. The sound of a remote being put down on a table. Heather finally turns her head toward us and slowly opens her eyes, REVEALING WHITE NOISE. She does not blink, blaring light and static sound toward us. We push in on her eyes, the cold frequency getting LOUDER, until we are in a choker, and then inside her, becoming her pupils, becoming the noise, becoming

Heather. Then there is no more

Heather,
just the frantic beads
of tingling pixels covering screen,
bringing us

into the story,
never fading out, never
cutting away.

# Abigail Nell

I ate too much bread.
I will never have the knees of Bardot
or the wives of Balanchine.
They must've had superior sartoriuses
to be with such a king.

Or is it sartori?
I prefer to think of my legs in Latin. This is a long, slow dance
with self-respect, and I lead with my clubbed foot.
Highfalutin and gluten free.

My stomach looks like uncooked pancake batter.
My upper thigh hangs over my kneecap like an old man's eyelid.
Imagine a Clydesdale hightailing it through Chinatown snow.
A chandelier covered in calk.

But I've crunched the numbers and think I've found my six-pack:
I'll get a new nose. The cartilage lost from one of those
can be measured in grams. If I shave my head,

that's shaving off one fourth of a pound.
66.6 percent of the three-pound human brain
would be another two pounds down.
The vestigiality of all phalanges is coming to an end.
So why keep them?
And twenty-five feet of intestinal tract?
Let's half that. Anything gastric's elastic.
Ribs can be replaced with plastic.

The femur bone is the largest and strongest in the human body.
It would take five times the amount of a person's weight to break it.
I don't plan on entering the Baby Elephant Bench Press Olympics.

I've already got a big upper lip, so why not
cut off the lower one, get rid of it?
Appendix and coccyx together weigh an infant.

I wonder about a weekly skin grafting treatment?
Skin: Who needs it?

I'll be the girl they say pink things to,
so weightless she arrives by ghost.

# Lupe Velez

Cast that bonita bitch pout,
that haughty hound pup strut,
that burned grapefruit breath,
that sexed headdress
poised with turquoise poison.

Cast that loca, better than "wild,"
shimmering brick-style, break through that
turn of the century's vaudevillian villainess turnstile.

Cast that stare that daze that spell that line
that part that hook that net that look,

that chair through a window
that brow arch, black as hell's rainbow.
That cha-cha leg language,
no para los gringos.

Cast that hypnotic beat of bone percussion.
Cast doubt.
Exotic leading ladies cast out.
Cast no more post-Barrymore.
That scripted last kiss with Harald Maresch, perished.

Cast that tone-deaf swan song,
that sound of an animal
being chased for its life in the night,
loud as the director yelling cut,
as the casket strapped to the back of the planet
whirling the mantra,
*Maria!*
*Maria!*
*Maria!*

# Taruni Sachdev

Pit the stars against her seizing heart;
let the best explosion win,
pull the worst man apart.

Not down for the count.
She's the punch that knocked the count out.

Loved beyond a reasonable doubt.
She's a tidal wave from a tiny spout,

a shutter speed on the lens
of an apparition's eye,
Lil bullied butterfly,

back into her cocoon,
relearning to fly.

# Julia Thorp

All thirteen years of him studied her question,
its clunky hooves floundering for traction
in the nascent dewy grooves of his snaking cortex.

(Remember when Artax got stuck in the swamp?
It was like that.)

He pulled out a matchbook, told her he'd give her the time
it took to burn the match gone to give
him three reasons why he should be her boyfriend.

*Well, we're almost the same age.*

*I love the things you say while playing basketball.*
*Obviously, I've seen all your games.*

*Our moms are really good friends.*

He handed her the coveted Yes,
she smiled, tucked it into her strut.
He watched her walk out of school
and into the front seat of a car
that was not her father's.

Remember when Artax disappeared into the swamp,
never to be seen by Atreyu again?
It was like that.

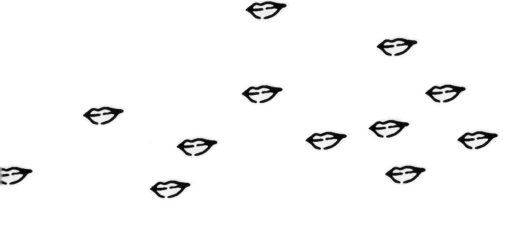

## Sharon Tate

Above me,
the blood thud packs its punches,
suitcases of adrenaline buck her stomach's structure,
my mother's.

A squirt of coral floods my cord,
flipping me breached,
the last onion
in a pickle jar.

A bright light passes over her rose wall,
rhubarb-colored vines and marbled sky
then dark again.

A finger pushes in.
A grumbled quake.

Then the thrash of light,
blades like ships crash through her vessels,
a celestial pattern,
the deep peepholes of God,
Little Dipper zippers opening her flesh.

This was how stars were made,
I was just there—
dabbing my pulp on the comets—
and now that thud's on ice,
and I feel my mother cooling,
me still inside her, forever.

# Marilyn Monroe

A fourth fret crept into the neck
of her index finger.

She had wound strands of blond too tightly.
A corpse corset of a capo.

It stayed like that: a rosy ring of jailed blood
that came to the barred window
and never left.

# Lindsay Lohan

# Jennifer Davis

Fame is the biological father of Pi.
3.14 we adore. Beyond that
the silence of Ever is what kills.
The never-ending necklace of decimals.

She stumbled across my genetic muck
saying *Hey, I'm Alison—do I know you
from somewhere? Are you famous
from something?* Yes, I'm from the center of

nowhere, performing Trapeze on a mane.
Tightrope-walking the telephone wires
of washed-up professional wrestlers.
I'm famous for my balance.

I had a cameo in the ninth pew of my father's funeral.
I starred in both Abandonments—
my mother's prequel, the sequel for my son.
I've been in the background my entire life.

Take it from an actress who never wanted to be one, Alison:
What I've been in and what you've been in
ain't nothin' compared to what we'll be in someday.
A fistfight with Heaven's entry fees.
A wolf prison when the moon finally throws us its bone.

A mediocre exchange of oxygenated vowels
with the landlords of our wrinkled tits.
Casting our sails into a body of acceptance
speeches with the lowest of tides.

Do you think you'll find me famous
when I tell you I'm broke?
When I tell you this drink is what keeps me going?
When I can't remember either what I was famous for.

Will I still be famous tomorrow when you wake up
and say to your roommate,
*I have discovered the final digit of Pi.*
*It's that drunk bitch in the Thirty-second Street bar.*

# Alison Andres

I couldn't remember her name, only that we are both specieless.
I recall some coded interview quote from the nineties
wearing too many auras, but even then she was impossible to read,
drowning in the glossy undercurrents of a magazine.

In person, she is a resistance of instances.
A rogue bud tastelessly wasting my tongue.

But her eyes.
Those hippodromes of grief.
I recognize their unsymmetrical trickle as my own,
her face an apron her mother left stains on.
Those slouched ducts, animated oilcans,
the parted beaks of birds bracing for lighting in trees.
Eyelashes long and straight as grass
on a dead man's lawn.

*There is no such throne* she said
when I asked if she was famous.
I sieved through the archives of her breath.

I wanted to say:
*Hey. I understand. I am an actress too.*

Tell her about the auditions and head shots,
rejection after long years of rejections,
notes about the lip I give,
surgical encouragements.

I wanted to attach my tipsy limbs to her umbilical,
reach in and untie all the knots,
turn them into safety nets for blood.

Instead, I walked away from the crash,
an upward-turned shield projecting
wrinkles onto my face.

My friends waited to hear what I'd uncovered.
I said nothing.

Ordered a hard drink, something darker, something I could see
my own reflection in.

# Rebecca Shaeffer

I turned up the volume on the TV,
let the laugh track eat the eggs
out of me. She set free
a thousand little boys
under my breath.
A rebirth. Of sorts.
My finger on the remote,
her hair my new midnight.
I could not obey curfews.
I would be her leading man.
She was my actress.
Off-screen I'd imagine
inviting her through the glass curtain,
letting her taste my knees.
I watched her grow up,
angels getting tangled in her fast ankles,
the slope of her earlobe must taste
of honeysuckled iron.

My beard tastes of fireplace-smoked fish.
I am watching myself grow old.
Cracking knees.
Through the glass curtain,
she is never on-screen anymore.
No actress.
Just leading men.
Her hair is becoming someone else's midnight.
New curfews.
New thumbs.
I wanted to cage a thousand boys

under her breath
in our final moments.
Make them a death. Of sorts.
Make a death of her.
But when I turn up the volume on the TV
no laugh track is playing.

# Elizabeth Pine

I wake to the throbbing
sounds of Ibiza on the television.

I see beautiful bikinis eating bananas.
In bikinis eating the asses
of other beautiful bikinis.

A girlie grind of tanned tibias.
Bronzed bombs ticking
twenty-four-karat beach backdrops.

Seems like everyone's having paradise for lunch but me.
I am no glowing globe of shaken gold.
No leggy Cindy. Kardashian't.

I am the crutch apparatus of an amputee.
The falsest identity. The girl next door
to the girl next door.

I'd like to dice up my eyes,
form a search party.

*We interrupt this program for breaking news:*

*Has anyone seen this nobody?*

# Dana Plato

My son spends all day polishing his weapon
before he pours the liquor in
and shoots himself in the mouth.

When his head is gone
the sky rains his remains for days.
His body stumbles around trying to steady itself.
His arms hold him upright, his hands
search for shelter.

Blasted, he'll dance on a dime
for strangers with quarters,
or mime a moment from Macbeth's death for paper.

When it stops raining,
I walk around and clean up his mess.
His blood on the bar,
the cement covered in meat.
His clothes, red ghosts,
his lungs hang from the trees.

At night I return to the home
we built from umbrellas.
I assemble his weapons, drink by drink.

Before I sleep,
I make a list of tomorrow's chores.
In the mirror I see only the time-
lapsed weather patterns of 1964.

## Samantha Smith

Out of the blue,
you rise like a bird shooting
through the Atlantic's attic.

What lifts you from the ocean cannot be seen.
It cannot be explained.

The plane crashed and now the splash grabs
up
for your feet to keep you in the deep

but you are free.

Your spine propels into daylight,
charging the tusks of clouds.

You are a gunpowder pilgrim.

You are no longer a child,
your voice no longer stuck
in the crashed black box that sunk in your gut,
no longer the flicker of someone else's desire,
higher now.

Up

Up

Now you owe the world nothing,
your heart catches up to your body and bleeds into sprint.

Up

Up

Now your mind obeys its outlaw,
all the broken clock hands want your time.
Not even the air can breathe
near your speed.

Up

Up

Now you're fourteen:

You love photographs,
particularly astrophotography,
something about the way the Hubble Telescope
can grasp the nth shades of red.

Seventeen:

You roll around in a bed of gardenia
with a boy named Henry who tells you
this is how they make perfume in Florence.

Twenty-one:

You see your first Broadway play
starring Vanessa Redgrave.
Her eyes are so familiar.

Twenty-five:

You beg your mother not to do anything to her face.
You tell her she's perfect.
You believe in her killer beauty
like Russians believe in ricin.

Twenty-nine:

You have so many questions to sow.

You cut off all your hair with kitchen scissors,
throw your favorite high heels
into the East River.

Thirty-two:

You study planets, Saturn's return.
Become obsessed with centrifugal force,
all known galaxies, physics,
the unknown heavens and hells.
Everything you cannot control.

Up

Up

Thirty-four:

You try on your first pressurized suit
during your astronautics exam.
You are in love.
You meet a man
who also defies gravity.

Thirty-five:

She is born with your mother's eyes.

Thirty-seven:

Your mother dies.

Forty-two:

On your first mission into space,
you recall your mother's umbilical cord
being cut from you.
Your high heels floating down the river,

all the way into the Atlantic Ocean.

Fifty-two:

Your daughter begs you not to do anything to your face.
You are perfect.

Up

Up

Higher now

Fifty-eight:

Sixty-three:

Sixty-five:

You take up guitar lessons before your last interstellar flight.
You write the only song you'll ever write.
About an actress's eyes.
How bold they were.
Bigger than Hepburn's.

Sixty-eight:

Your daughter has so many questions to sow.
Your answers are in full bloom.

Seventy-five:

No longer a child—

Eighty-one:

not even the air can breathe—

Ninety-three:

The Earth grabs

up

up

up

up

up

for your feet—

but what lifts you from this world
cannot be seen

you are free

you are free

you are free

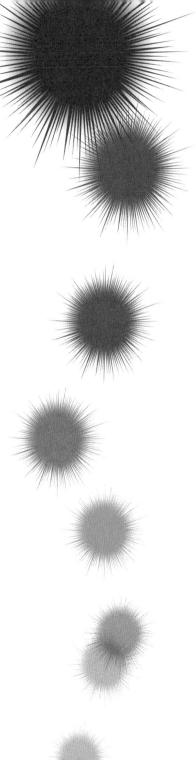

# Lucy Gordon

In the paraphrased haze of hash I ask about Lucy.
Not what was written in the Guardian
but what you've been guarding.

We are so high, the moon is in your mouth, it's hard to articulate
your mourning. Grief tugs in all directions on each tooth.
Your knees touch like the foreheads of sole surviving siblings.

The Lucy the Guardian knew
was from London, was beautiful and talented.
Born 1980.

*The Lucy I knew,* you begin,
*Carried all her secrets in her hands.*
*They were so quiet.*

She went to Oxford and spoke French fluently. Her parents were
middle-class academics. *One of her parents was a shrink.* She moved
to New York to pursue modeling, *liked to smoke cigarettes at Lucky
Strike. She was chased by creatures* and men adored her.

*Once, she paid for her parents to stay at the Soho Grand when they
came to visit. They were embarrassed she paid. She was embarrassed
they were embarrassed.*
A cab came whizzing by with her face on it. Her parents were thrilled.
*She cried.*

*They eventually got divorced. Her mother got cancer.* Lucy threw
herself into work *to* *outrun the guilt of not being there.* She segued into
acting, *a kind of bladed snake that slithered into existing wounds.* She
was excited *and anxious* for her first big film. She went to its premiere,
*where the director told her she had been cut out of the film.*

She sat and watched, smiling.

*Some of her eating issues came back.* Lucy got a shrink. Was treated for depression. *My buddy Neil swears she started talking about herself in the third person around this time. There was a fresh desperation. She would fall instantly in love with anyone she met on a plane. She was so English about not showing what was going on inside.*

She moved to Los Angeles to pursue more work *when we met. Our lives were going nowhere. I had PTSD. She was lost. We would drive around listening to Otis Redding box sets and eat pie and drink coffee in the middle of the night at diners.*

She loved *rosé and shellfish and the sound of rain on windows.* She was *very* comfortable *to lay my head on* in her new apartment. *She had two veins that formed a V in the middle of her forehead whenever she laughed or sighed.*

*Something amazing could be happening between us she said.*

*I shut down inside shut her down outside*

*We didn't talk for a while.*

Lucy moved to France and met a cinematographer whom she *quickly* moved in with. *Lost.* She became close with his family and his daughter, *especially his mother. Lucy loved the way she held pens. Her quiet hands. Her green glass vases, spread around the house, holding nothing.*

She was cast as Jane Birkin in the Serge Gainsbourg biopic.

*The mother became ill.*

Months later, Lucy went to Cannes with her costar to promote their film.

*Something happened*

*Lost*

*Outrun the guilt*

*With a smile on her face*

She came home from Cannes *to help her boyfriend bury his mother. The death was quick.*

A friend in England committed suicide.

*Her mother was still ill back in England.*

*The guilt.*

*I rang her in Paris to check in.*
*It was a Monday.*
*She needed to call me back.*

Was from London

Beautiful and talented

Born 1980

–2009.

The cinematographer found her and screamed for the police. *In his desperation to revive her with CPR, he broke three of her ribs. This is how he knew for sure she was dead.*

"Acting is what she always wanted to do. It's a tragedy that it's been cut off so soon."

"Lucy brought light. She was bright in every moment of her life."

"                              ," they said.

"                     ," she was quoted as saying.

"                            ," the statement from the family read.


*I helped Lucy's sister clean out her apartment in the East Village three weeks later.*

Lucy Gordon left her estate to friends, family, and her sister.

*She wore Lucy's clothes the entire time we packed.*
*Her quiet hands, filling up boxes,*
*inviting all the silence to finally leave the room.*

# Barbara La Marr

(323) 469-9933

# Laurel Gene

Shave the sheets of my songless success,
expose the rotted age of me now—
my toothless breasts, my hips like a cracked cow skull
hanging crooked on the butcher's wall.

Remember what I once was.
The laurels of the Gene name.
My boom impact on the Baby Generation.
My prepubescent niche pizzazz.

Remember how the phone threw offers for
Little Jenny Sues into my father's ear. He'd
suck the bucks out of the cord,
a straw into a spectrogram.

I was his dark sparkler. A tarantula on fire.
An innocent with apple juice eyes and a
brain full of famished birds.

I used to play characters. Now I'm portrayed.
As a thirty-year-old eighty-year-old domestic darling.
My husband's office phone plays mum. The only offers are
from the sink's silverfish to kill them.

When I vacuum I think of Ingmar Bergman
fucking me from behind. I open
like the palms of Julius Caesar to a crowd.
Men used to rearrange their months to fit my seasons.

I suck a finger then the cauldron in his tip.
He films my apron sticking to the sweat.
Makes this bad heart a pulse from the sky.

I am a distant explosion of myself
again. A star. Remember

being a star.

This is how to die in the arms of a suburban wind,
learning how to be forgotten
over and over again.

# Frances Farmer

## 1.

The doctors spent ten years working on flower arrangements
in the boned vase that held up her brain.

When she came out, you could see through her skin to the frozen pipes.

Her fingernails were green boats beached into their mossed beds.

At the movie premiere, she dragged a leg behind her.
Walked on the side of her ankle in front of the photographers.

*Frances!* they'd clamor,
*Tell your fans how you keep such a trim figure!*

Her eyes cooked like the fresh campfires
of convicts on the run.

Everyone loved her new hairstyle—
two oiled fish skins parted down the middle.

*Frances!*
*Tell us what you've been up to all these years!*
*What was it like to work with Tyrone Power?*

Frances opened her mouth to answer
A bug crawled out, fell to the ground
and burrowed right back into a hole in her foot.

The paparazzi followed her every move,
taking shots of liquid
she'd leave behind.

They loved the beads
of blood she wore down her neck.

The yellow diamonds
crusted in her eyes.

The tie-dye trend of
immortal death. To die forever.

After an embrace, her lover found himself
leaning down
to pick up all her bones off the ground.

## 2.
Mr. Harvester came home one evening and found a trail
of withered deer thighs on his front lawn.

Mrs. Pellington found muddy footprints leading up her front porch
and only muddy handprints leading away from it.

An old roommate of Christine swore she saw someone
climb a telephone pole one night to eat pigeon eggs from their nests.

Rumor had it someone had been stealing chicken hearts
from the Branson Family Butchery.

The Weintraubs in 4B went missing, completely.

All the children knew better.
Something was strange
about the fleshed thing
that lived at the end of their street.

One of the children,
a young boy named Bruce,
called her *Francestein.*

*Francestein.*

### 3.

Bruce and his mother sat in the living room
watching an episode of *This Is Your Life*.

The guest, Frances Farmer, listened to the voice of a surprise guest
who would reveal himself as an old friend.
The old friend ran out onto the stage
and threw his arms around Frances.
The audience applauded.

Frances mirrored the man,
doing as he did,
moving her arms
in his way,
feeling as he felt.

Bruce watched her nose
sniff at the side of the friend's head,
her tongue like a worm, searching
for a way in.

# Quentin Dean

Was last seen in the last scene
of "A Person Unknown."

Could be overheard offering lasso lessons
to the mortician on his day off.

Kept a box of black widow spiders as pets.
Fed them fresh aphids from the bellies of calla lilies.

Once poured a bottle of Campari in the kiddie pool,
dared Patrick to dive.

Broke my brother's heart
like the shell of an egg between meals.

Never spoke of it again.

Insisted we make the soup from scratch.

Told us if we wanted to fly in our dreams
we must eat cayenne pepper before bed.

Had a doppelgänger in Nebraska
who sketched missing horses for a living.

Took too many mushrooms one summer, spent an afternoon reading
Scripture and Meisner leaning over
an ice tray in the freezer.

Sent a care package of bologna packed with frozen books.

Sent all the historians thank-you notes on stationery
bearing their mothers' names.

Sent her biographer to a mental institution.

Kissed me in a neon alley in fake Paris.

In between Russian roulette's bullets.

All up against the fortune-teller's window.

Walked the walk.
Talked the dirty talk.

Tongue-tied the sword swallower,
made a cherry stem out of him.

Never tied the knot.

Had four children.
Was survived by three children.

Went by the name Andrea.

Was also known as Palmer.

Will be remembered as Dolores.

A.k.a. Corky.

Gave me the nickname Blue Kid.

Is still alive.

Never lived.

# Epilogue

## *True or False:*

The actress
The batshit catalyst
The spoiled brat
The narcissist
Mommy's child
Bonnie's employer
The most selfish friend
The indecisive twentysomething
The ambitious auditioner
The adult ingenue
The space case
The one who is always late
The flake
The girlfriend you can't count on
The girlfriend you can take advantage of
The self-absorbed whiner
The gutless tearjerker
The stunted mirror lurker
The same ol' same ol'
The one who got away
The one who is going away
The fiery liar
The uninspired for hire
The networker extraordinaire
The soul-broke millionaire
The horror movie captivator
The serial masturbator
The serial cereal eater
The best fucking kisser
The second best fuck since Tinder

78

The temper igniter
The nameless woman
Amber Tamblyn
The abortionist
The fortuneless extortionist
The breadwinner
The dead ringer
Fake Emma Stone
The poet
The author
died during the writing of this book.

### Facts about Brittany Murphy for Poem journal entry June 22, 2010

- She died in the shower.

- Her film *Uptown Girls* grossed $44,617,342.

- Her film *Abandoned* was released posthumously, straight to DVD.

- My old agent told me no one was allowed to call her house before 10:00 A.M.

- She was 5' 2" tall.

- She was diagnosed with a heart murmur as a child.

- She was dropped from the film *Happy Feet* due to rumored drug abuse.

- Her cause of death was pneumonia.*

- Brittany wrote poetry.

I took a break from writing about the dead
and drinking from writing about the dead
to walk around my childhood neighborhood.
Everything's for rent. Or for sale, for ten
times the amount it's worth.

Palm trees are planted in front of a mural
of palm trees under the Ocean Park Bridge.
In the painting, the metal horses of a carousel are breaking
free and running down the beach. Why didn't I leave

my initials in cement
in front of my parents' apartment in the eighties?
Nikki had the right idea in '79.

I walk by a basketball court, where men play
under the fluorescent butts of night's cigarette.
I could have been any of their wives,
at home, filling different rooms in different houses
with hopeful wombs. Agreeing on paint color

samples with their mothers in mind.
I'll bet their wives let their cats go out
hunting at night like premonitions of future sons.
They will worry, stare out the front window,
pray that privilege doesn't bring home bad news
like some wilted head of a black girl in nascent jaws.

To say nothing of the owl who's been here for years. I hear him

when I'm trying to write about the deaths I've admired.
I hear him when the clothed me no longer recognizes
the naked. I hear him while writing and shitting and sleeping
where my mother's seven guitars sleep.
I hear him in my parents' house,

their walls covered in my many faces,
traces of decades of complacence.

My childhood neighborhood is a shrine to my success,
and I'm a car with a bomb inside, ready
to pull up in front of it and stop
pretending.

From:    Amber Rose ███████████████████████

to:       Mindy Nettifee████████████████████████

date:    Tue, Jan 12, 2009 at 1:27 PM

subject:  Saturn's return.

. . . I know this is gonna be a bad year for me. Last year was a bad year for all my friends and I felt for them. And I felt mine coming. And here it is. I'm just going to embrace it and hope a spark ignites.

I think I could very possibly be heading toward a full-scale breakdown in the next few months. I know, this is out of nowhere, right? I've been hiding it, I think. Even from myself. I am so creatively low and impotent, I know I have to make a move but in what direction . . . I don't know. Where do I start? Get rid of Mom's tchotchkes in my house? Get rid of ████? Fire my agency? Go to London with David for a month and get some clarity or come back to L.A. for a month and find some clarity? What the fuck is clarity? Can I just go the way of Brittany Murphy and say fuck it, do drugs until I drop and call it a day? What's the point of taking care of yourself if you don't even care about yourself? . . .

# Great Names for Fake Actresses 2009

Linda Liftstrom

Ivory Soapra

Jan Power Strength

Maple Tomahockette

Rasputina

Iwana Oscar

Mesmerelda Burn

Shiver Softgold

I passed
but it was offered to me
but I passed
I was heavily considered for it
I killed in the room
but they went in a different direction
my agent couldn't get to it
she had to be at Amy Adams's baby shower
but if I manage expectations in my thirties
one day my agent might send an Edible Arrangement
to *my* baby shower
like Sam What's His Face did for me
after *The Grudge 2* soared in dollar bills
but sank in reviews.

When I went to Japan to shoot that film,
the director asked me to lose weight
through his interpreter. Every day I ate
the ironed meat and beard clippings of an iceberg wedge
off the bread of a Subway sandwich.

I should've passed
but it was offered to me
but I should have
an actress who is very famous now
was heavily considered for it then
she killed in the room
but they went in a different direction
her agent couldn't get to it
the agent had to be at my poetry reading
but the actress managed expectations
in her twenties
and one day all the agents sent her rare orchids

and licked the stiff slits of her red carpet genius
and poured Up and Coming
all over my Down and Going

the auction of our bodies
passing each other by
between buyers' hands
down and going
going
gone.

From:     Amber Rose ████████████████████
to:     "tamblyn, russ" ████████████████████
date:     Thu, Apr 26, 2012 at 6:36 PM
subject:  Papa.

I hope that you are not disappointed in me.
I hope you aren't taking this show not happening
    as hard as I'm taking it.
I need you to not give up in believing in me.
I need you to help me believe in myself.
I need you to not hit the bottle and stare at the television and be
    depressed the way I am going to do tonight.
I need you to be strong for me. Strong in the way that perhaps, when
    you ever felt like a failure, you could not be for yourself.
I need you to toast Mom to all that I have done in this short lifetime
    and say, my time will come.

I love you

*Updated 2014: Cause of death, possible homicide by poisoning.

### Facts about Dana Plato for Poem December 2011

- Her film *Pacino Is Missing* was never released.

- She was fired from *Diff'rent Strokes* after becoming pregnant.

- Dana appeared on Howard Stern's radio program, where callers assailed her with comments like *has-been*.

- Dana died of a drug-overdosed suicide the next day in her mother's RV. It was Mother's Day.

- A friend of Shappy's has a recording of a frantic Dana Plato on a tape from an old message machine. She left it the day before she died.

- Dana's son committed suicide almost exactly twenty-five years later. It was Mother's Day.

- My birthday often falls on Mother's Day. It is always the day before my mother's birthday.

I'm the war I want
to end.

A woman of her word
not spoken.

I'm the war I want
to end.

Alone in my house, burning
all the wood and the bridges.

I'm the war I want
to end.

The persona, My Sharona,
phony bologna.

I'm the war I want
to end.

*You're good for nothing*
*and nothing's good for you.*

I'm the war I want
to end.

James Franco says
write me off like a sunsetting trend.

But that's not a war I want
to start.

That's the war he wants
to pretend.

I'm the war I want
to end.

From:      Amber Rose █████████████████
to:           Beau Sia ███████████████
date:      Thu, Apr 26, 2012 at 6:28 PM
subject:  Here is what I started writing to Mindy

. . . I am ashamed to admit that I hate myself so much as to look in the eyes of the man I love and hate him for loving me today. To pity his love of such a failure. If I could close my eyes right now and never open them again, I would. I would do that.

I'm trying to write your poem, Martha Mansfield. But I can't
memorize your lines. You are the last on my list of actresses. The
last one owed her ode. Something about a hoop skirt that caught on
fire in 1923 and seared an epitaph into our memories. Only no one
remembers you, respectfully. No one will remember me, either. We're
last spring's birds' nests. We're the venison at the steak dinner. That's
all I got. I'm fresh out of sober soliloquies.
No more metaphors, no more similes. (See how I did that?)

Let me search you on Wikipedia, see if I can find some oil for the
engine. But before I do, how about another pat on the ass for this glass
of comatose that's roofied my throat? Do you think maybe Charles
Bukowski once drank this same thing and said that same thing, only
without red lipstick? I took a half of a half of a little pill, Martha, I
must confess. Now the keyboard's letters are so soft. Double-you. Eye.
Kay. Eye. So this is what it would feel like to run fingers over the top
of rush-hour traffic! That long school bus space bar. The little black
limos and hearses at either end, celebrating in their own ways. The
keyboard feels like a thousand silk tiles. Like the tops of a hundred
baby tarps at an Ant Art Fair.
Pea. Ee. Dee. Eye. Ay.

It says you'd wanted to be an actress since the age of fourteen. When
I turned fourteen, Martha, I wanted to retire from acting. I had
already lived so much. I got my belly button pierced and crashed my
parents' car. A guy went down on me for the first time. He had a labret
piercing. I had slender arms, long and soft like a stream of milk into
a baby's mouth. I was young. Now I'm just still young. I had a baby's
face. Now I'm just baby-faced.

One night at a Hollywood party I met Leonardo DiCaprio. Think
Buster Keaton, only minus some bravery. Leo didn't flirt with me that
night. I lined my lips with brown eyeliner like the cholas I grew up
with in Venice Beach and wore a choker of silver plastic stars around

my neck. I wasn't his type. He wasn't mine. But we did dance together for a few minutes. He in his black shirt and backward baseball cap, me in cargo pants and a red tube top. Shit, you probably don't know what that is, Martha. It's like a tiara for your tits.

After the party, my friends and I picked up some wannabes and some wannados, minus Leo, though I think a friend of his ended up with us. I don't remember how we all got to the beach from there but the wind was in our favor, the amateur tequila throwing up in our buckets. We picked up another guy from the party who was even younger than us, who smelled like lemonade aftershave. His eyes were big sapphires resting in platinum cheeks. His grandmother must've been Elizabeth Taylor, we were certain. Our coreless trunks struck partial headstands in the shifting billions of beige, and our bras played fetch with the jaws of the Pacific. A sand-ball fight seemed like the right plan. Our only towels, each other's clothes. We slid onward and over ourselves, toward the light of the pier, toward the frozen fireworks and whatever might be coming next. I was hanging on to Not Leo, and another friend—Sonya I think her name was—clung onto the night's biceps, testing our curfew's strength. And you, Martha, making us laugh, pointing a finger at the crooked pier pillars holding up the rickety wood extension. "Don't sneeze," you commanded. "The whole thing might collapse in an explosion of air hockey pucks and baby shoes!" Your white dress crystallized with seawater, your plum waist belt now in your hand, dragging through the foam behind you like a soft tail.

Remember how you took us under the pier, where lovers and homeless huddled in a unified effort for warmth? In the low violet light, I searched a boy's face for lips and leaned into my first kiss. I opened my eyes for a moment and saw you over his shoulder. When I closed them and felt his soft mouth splash into mine, our salts not saved for the sea, I imagined I was kissing you, Martha. I was kissing you.

"He can tell you can and will write 'blammo' poems (I told him I'd quote him), but that these were not them (for him)."

—Rejection letter from well-known publication

"You should write under a pseudonym. People will take you more seriously."

—*Well-known older male poet from New York City,*
*over a plate of expensive cheeses*

Dear men in Congress,
You think banning birth control is conservative progress?
You think sanctioning my ovaries won't bring me to violence?
How about I tell you what to do with your caucus?

It is now illegal to think about me topless.
To keep your lotion where your socks is.
To refer to powerful women as monsters like those jocks at Fox did.

I am not afraid to cock block dick,
to sew an instructional video for rape kits to your eyelids and make
    you
watch it,

I'll take away your golf clubs and gun clips,
I'm gonna fix this by getting YOU fixed!

Enough's enough, kid,
come on stop that,
if you want to make this Law
then here's my Law Rap:
You have the right to get strangled by a bra strap,
anything you sexualize with can and will get shot at
with a Glock cap,

I'll shove your life in a duffel bag,
hand it over to a sex trafficker, let him smuggle that.

You wanna cuddle, Dad?

NO

DON'T TOUCH ME

YOU CAN'T TOUCH ME ANYMORE!

I'M SO PISSED I FORGOT HOW TO RHYME

I HATE YOU SO MUCH I FORGOT
WHAT I WAS TALKING ABOUT

WHO WANTS TO GET MEXICAN FOOD?
JAY-Z DO SOMETHING!

I am the single white female of
you
die
in
the
end.

This
is do or die
these are the new rules I play by
this is the end of the line, k, old white guy?

Ladies testify
it's time to put a measure on the floor
against chromosome Y

All
In favor
Say

I,

Amber Rose Tamblyn, of sound body and mind, do solemnly swear, upon and into this great day numbered twenty-one of such and such month in the year two thousand and tweeelve, to finish this book and these poemies, so help me the cast of *The Help*. But prior to such suchyness, I bequeath, bestow, and nudge gently with offering my every fortune to this bottle of aged bourbon, that browned-downer, that silkless lung humper, that unlawful talk-softener, that best friend of THE FUCKING COPS (I'll punch you right in the cork, old-timer!). And in this estate thine shalt find the following: my many remotes for my one TV, a funny-looking pair of socks purchased in the great state of Utah, that box of childhood report cards I promised my mom I would go through, my absolutely unwavering terror about the wedding, and the remaining muscle relaxers I dare not take tonight, nay, given unto me by a guy named Ned. Those sleepy sternum steepers, those fun hunters, those actress, smacktressters.

Amen? Sign here.

## March 24, 2013

*Hi, I was supposed to send these flowers*
*to something called a "wife"?*
*If you are this person, please enjoy and reply*
*with a definition. David.*

Wife: Someone who is a female partner
   in a continuing marital relationship.

Someone who thinks that definition better defines you, actually.

Someone who loves your love for obscure British satire zines.

Someone who looks through your old pictures
and tells you she would make love
to every era of you.
Even the underage ones.

Someone who likes to make things weirder than you do.

Someone who isn't afraid to tell you how you really feel
about that one Woody Allen movie.

Someone who looks forward to fifty more years
of explaining basic directions to you.

No, really.

Someone who likes watching you
watch Guy Maddin films.

Someone who thinks your period jokes are funny,
but not in front of her feminist friends.
That's no fun for everyone.

Someone who loves that you want her

to pick out your new spectacles
because she is the one who will have to look at them every day.

Someone who is not afraid to write in the third person
because she lives in the third person, for a living.

Someone who can never get enough of your love
for bands that came out of Boston in the nineties.

Someone who needs the way you kiss.
The way you graze on a lip like straw
in the mouth of a Southern kid.

Someone who watched you help a blind man at a festival
so he wouldn't miss the band reunion of Jesus Lizard,
even though all your fans wouldn't leave you alone.

Someone who will never leave you
alone.

Someone only you could make laugh
during a documentary about the Holocaust,
during sex,
during study breaks of the bleakest women.

Someone you said "Don't get obsessed" to after the first poem,
knowing full well she would.

Knowing full well,
it's how you became
hers.

Search "Famous actress ghost continues to haunt local town"
Search "Biographies of actresses in the film 'Poltergeist' + Dead"
Search "Origin of a curse"
Search "Baby from famous commercial dies"
Search "Deceased actresses under 30"
Search "Death certificate for Quentin Dean"
Search "YouTube + Quentin Dean interview"
Search "YouTube + Emily Quartermaine 1995"
Search "Amber Tamblyn + news"
Search "Amber Tamblyn + bad poetry"
Search "The worst celebrity poets"
Search "IMDb + Best actresses under 30"
Search "IMDb + most underrated actresses over 30"
Search "Screen Actors Guild statistics + how many actresses work past
   age 30"
Search "Fay DeWitt + murder"
Search "Iranian actress Asal Badiee + murdered?"
Search "How to identify human poisoning + homicide"
Search "Brittany Murphy autopsy + hair sample test"
Search "How many hairs are on the human head?"
Search "Brittany Spears shaves head"
Search "Rotten Tomatoes + Crossroads movie"
Search "Different spellings for the name Brittany"
Search "Origin of the name Britney"
Search "Other British namesakes"
Search "Jean Seberg"
Search "Self-induced drug poisoning"
Search "Difference between Demerol and Percocet"
Search "Order Percocet online"
Search "How to clear your search history"
Search "Whitney Houston + drug overdose"
Search "Rotten Tomatoes + The Bodyguard movie"

Search "Statistics on premature obituaries"
Search "Whitney Houston false drug overdose obit after 9/11"
Search "Actress killed at World Trade Tower"
Search "Actresses who died in planes"
Search "Pop singer Aaliyah"
Search "Rotten Tomatoes + Romeo Must Die movie"
Search "Rotten Tomatoes + Amber Tamblyn movies"
Search "Unknown actresses and actors of vaudeville"
Search "Eddie Tamblyn + brain tumor"
Search "Unknown actress deaths"
Search "National Archives + Actresses, deceased"
Search "Manjula died age 35"
Search "Geeta Bali died age 34"
Search "Lilian Velez died age 24"
Search "Liliana Lozano died age 30"
Search "Clarine Seymour died age 21 + unmarked grave"
Search "Adriana Prieto died age 24"
Search "Shobha died age 17"
Search "Inger Stevens died age 35"
Search "Marjie Millar died age 34 + fourteen surgeries on left leg"
Search "Billie Carleton died age 22"
Search "Silk Smitha died age 35"
Search "Masako Natsume died age 27"
Search "Nina Byron died age unknown"
Search "Romina Yan died age 36 + sudden death"
Search "Zou Xuan died age 39"
Search "Suzzy Williams died age 23"
Search "Soundarya died age 31 + plane crash"
Search "Li Tobler died age 27 + suicide"
Search "Vincenza Armani died age 39"
Search "Daniella Perez died age 22"
Search "Corrona Riccardo died age 39"
Search "Marilyn Miller died age 37 + complications with nasal surgery"

Search "Rebecca Shaeffer died age 21 + murdered + stalker + Robert John Bardo"
Search "Dominique Dunne died age 22 + murdered + boyfriend + John Thomas Sweeney"
Search "Mary Thurman died age 30"
Search "Jang Jin-Young died age 37 + life imitates art"
Search "Evelyn Nelson died age 23"
Search "Gaby Deslys died age 38 + carved wood swan bed"
Search "Florence La Badie died age 29"
Search "Peg Entwistle died age 24 + jumped to death from HOLLYWOODLAND sign"
Search "Krista Nell died age 29"
Search "Florence Barker died age 21"
Search "Carole Landis died age 29 + Seconal + suicide + Rex Harrison"
Search "Anissa Jones died age 18 + Seconal + overdose + doctor prescribed"
Search "Madhubala died age 36 + VSD + hole in heart"
Search "Candy Darling died age 29"
Search "Corinne Luchaire died age 28 + association with German occupation"
Search "Renee Adoree died age 35"
Search "Valentina Zimina died age 29"
Search "Zoe Tamerlis Lund died age 37"
Search "Thelma Todd died age 29 + carbon monoxide"
Search "Meena Kumari died age 39"
Search "Elizabeth Rachel Felix died age 36"
Search "Iris Stuart died age 33"
Search "Françoise Dorleac died age 25 + body identified by diary and checkbook"
Search "Valerie Quennessen died age 31"
Search "Jean Harlow died age 26 + renal failure"
Search "Alma Rubens died age 33"

Search "Mahua Roychoudhury died age 27"

Search "Gladys Brockwell died age 35"

Search "Lya De Putti died age 34 + chicken bone removed from throat"

Search "Myrtle Gonzalez died age 27"

Search "Marie-Georges Pascal died age 39"

Search "Roxanne Kernohan died age 32"

Search "Marie Prevost died age 38 + acute alcoholism"

Search "Soledad Miranda died age 27"

Search "Nell Gwyn died age 37"

Search "Sammi Kane Kraft died age 20"

Search "Monal died age 21"

Search "Lucy Gordon died age 28 + suicide + hanging"

Search "Gail Russell died age 36"

Search "Barbara Payton died age 39"

Search "Frances Farmer died age 56 + shock therapy + alcoholism + abortion + cancer"

Search "Iday Hawley died age 32"

Search "Lillian Peacock died age 28"

Search "Dorothy Stratten died age 20 + rape + crime of passion"

Search "Donyale Luna died age 33"

Search "Dorrit Weixler died age 24"

Search "Virginia Rappe died age 30 + Fatty Arbuckle"

Search "Evelyn Preer died age 36"

Search "Gloria Grey died age 38"

Search "Allyn King died age 31 + jumpers who survive"

Search "Francelia Billington died age 39"

Search "Debbie Weems died age 27"

Search "Susan Peters died age 31 + gunshot + paralysis + anorexia + kidney disease"

Search "Pepi Lederer died age 25"

Search "Susan Littler died age 34"

Search "Florence Deshon died age 28 + gas poisoning"
Search "Charlotte Long died age 18"
Search "Janet Banzet died age 37 + Marie Brent + Pat Barnett + Patricia Barrett+ Pat Barrett + Anne Brent + Louise Brent"
Search "Agnes Souret died age 26"
Search "Marietta Millner died age 34 + anorexia"
Search "Marilyn Miller died age 37"
Search "Ogarita Elizabeth Bellows died age 32 + daughter of John Wilkes Booth"
Search "Diana Sands died age 39"
Search "Rosamond Pinchot died age 33"
Search "Dorothy Hale died age 33"
Search "Pascal Olier died age 25"
Search "Barbara La Marr died age 29 + tuberculosis + nephritis"
Search "Peggy Shannon died age 34"
Search "Susanne Cramer died age 32"
Search "Carol Haney died age 39 + Gene Kelly protégée"
Search "Taya Straton died age 36"
Search "Pauline Chan Bo-Lin died age 29"
Search "Joan Dowling died age 26"
Search "Karyn Kupcinet died age 22 + homicide possibly linked to assassination of JFK"
Search "Jessica Madison Wright died age 21"
Search "Jeanette Loff died age 35"
Search "Laura Addison died age 30 + shipwreck"
Search "Michele Girardon died age 36"
Search "Emily Hogquist died age 34"
Search "Rasika Joshi died age 38"
Search "Pauline Lafont died age 25 + hiking accident"
Search "Gloria Dickson died age 27"
Search "Edith Roberts died age 35 during childbirth"
Search "Diana Miller died age 25"

Search "Sirkka Sari died age 19 + fell down chimney into furnace"

Search "Bai Jing died age 28"

Search "Suzi Lovegrove died age 32 + HIV positive born"

Search "Divya Bharti died age 19"

Search "Jeanne Eagels died age 39"

Search "Suzanna Sablairolles died age 37"

Search "Bridgette Andersen died age 21 + Savannah Smiles + heroin + alcohol"

Search "Shannon Michelle Wilsey died age 23 + Savannah + suicide"

Search "Dorothy Seastrom died age 26"

Search "Aileen Marson died age 26"

Search "Samantha Smith died age 13 + plane crash + USSR"

Search "Viveka Babajee died age 37"

Search "Marguerite Marsh died age 37"

Search "Karen Jonsson died age 33 + fatalities pre penicillin"

Search "Betty Morrissey died age 36"

Search "Amber Tamblyn died age        "

Search "Lottie Lyell died age 35"

Search "Sophie Heathcote died age 33"

Search "Renate Muller died age 31 + Nazi conspiracy"

Search "Sidney Fox died age 30"

Search "Vanessa Cavanagh died age 18 + car accident"

Search "Aleena died age 20 or 21 + unknown DOB"

Search "Heather O'Rourke died age 12 + stenosis + cardiac arrest"

Search "Pisith Pilika died age 34"

Search "Jill Banner died age 35"

Search "Yumika Hayashi died age 35 + Japan's biggest porn star"

Search "Ruth Eweler died age 34"

Search "Marie-Soleil Tougas died age 27"

Search "Taruni Sachdev died age 14 + plane crash"

Search "Iren Agay died age 38"

Search "Mabel Hite died age 29"

Search "Sharon Tate died age 26 + murder + Manson family"

Search "Jiah Khan died age 25"

Search "June Thorburn died age 36"

Search "Meenakshi Thapar died age 27+ kidnapped + decapitated"

Search "Sheree Winton died age 39"

Search "Thuy Trang died age 27"

Search "Sonia Martinez died age 30 + early AIDS in Spain"

Search "Asal Badiee died age 35"

Search "Mandi Lampi died age 19"

Search "Adelaide Neilson died age 32 + ruptured fallopian tube"

Search "Julie Vega died age 16"

Search "Aleta Freel died age 28 + suicide by gunshot"

Search "Lily Hanbury died age 34"

Search "Trinity Loren died age 34"

Search "Laura Sadler died age 22 + fell off a building"

Search "Merna Kennedy died age 36"

Search "Carole Lesley died age +38"

Search "Jean Stuart died age 20 + horseback riding accident"

Search "Su Muy Key died age 21 or 22 + unknown DOB"

Search "Marilyn Monroe died age 36 + overdose"

Search "Guylaine St-Onge died age 39"

Search "Thelma Hill died age 31"

Search "Adrienne Ames died age 39"

Search "Lupe Velez died age 36 + Seconal + suicide"

Search "Janet Munro died age 38"

Search "Mary Lawson died age 30 + WWII bombing in London"

Search "Lucille Ricksen died age 14"

Search "Shiho Niiyama died age 29"

Search "Kay Kendall died age 32 + leukemia + married to Rex
  Harrison lied"

Search "Sophie Gimber Kuhn died age +28"

Search "Leila Diniz died age 27"

Search "Selena died age 23 + murdered by fan"

Search "Marjorie White died age 31"

Search "Diane Linkletter died age 20"
Search "Miss Kumari died age 37"
Search "Feri Cansel died age 39"
Search "Claudette Mawby died age 20 + WWII bombing in Brighton"
Search "Debbie Linden died age 36"
Search "Virginia Maskell died age 31 + postpartum depression"
Search "Paola Pezzaglia died age 36"
Search "Sibyl Sanderson died age 37"
Search "Julia Dean died age 37 + childbirth"
Search "Anna Maria de Bruyn died age 36"
Search "Chane't Johnson died age 34"
Search "Lya De Putti died age 34 + Harbor Sanitorium"
Search "Jean Gillie died age 33"
Search "Ebba Morman died age 33 + tuberculosis"
Search "Quentin Dean died age 58 + ?"
Search "Sriranjani died age 33"
Search "Sunny Johnson died age 30 + burst blood vessel in her brain"
Search "Misty Upham died age 32 + police negligence—the woods"
Search "Funny cat videos"

From:     Amber Rose █████████████████████
to:         ███████████████████
date:     Sat, Dec 28, 2013 at 9:13 AM
subject:   Inquiry

Hi there,
My name is Amber Tamblyn and I am a poet and actress from New York and Los Angeles. I am currently working on a poem about Fay for my next collection of poems about the lives and deaths of child-star actresses, which will be published by HarperCollins in 2015. I wanted to know if it might be possible to interview Ms. DeWitt? So as to be transparent, I would need to ask about the 1965 incident involving Ray Allen. From a writing perspective, I'm interested in Fay's life before and after this incident, told by her—how she felt and how it changed her—rather than reading an article about it. Ms. DeWitt is the antithesis of what I have studied in many regards and I'm interested in her story. I imagine this might be a sensitive subject, but I assure you I am not a reporter and have no intention to paint her untruthfully. I hope she might consider it.

Thanks for taking the time to read this and happy holidays,

*Amber Tamblyn*

From:      Stage 9 Talent ████████████
to:        Amber Rose ██████████████
date:      Sat, Dec 28, 2013 at 10:57 PM
subject:   Re: Inquiry

From:    Amber Rose ███████████████
to:        Stage 9 Talent ███████████████
date:      Sun, Dec 29, 2013 at 6:53 PM
subject:   Re: Inquiry

Sorry—there was a reply from you but no message. Did you intend to have a message for me?

Thanks,

Amber

Did you intend to have a message for me?

## *Definition of MEMENTO MORI:*

A reminder of mortality.

ORIGIN: Latin.

Translation:

*Remember that you must die.*

From:     Russ Tamblyn ▓▓▓▓▓▓▓▓▓▓▓
to:     Amber Tamblyn ▓▓▓▓▓▓▓▓▓▓▓▓
date:     Thu, Apr 26, 2012 at 7:45 PM
subject:   RE: Papa.
to me

I'm over it! You just were not supposed to do this show. I KNOW something even better will come along. Hopefully, a comedy.

Please don't feel bad about it. That is not where you're supposed to be. Your time will DEFINITELY come again and I believe in you emphatically!

So much love to you.

# Acknowledgments

Starting from the beginning: Thank you Roxane Gay, Rachel Mckibbens, and Mindy Nettifee for planting the seeds. Thank you Beau Sia, Derrick Brown, Janet Fitch, Jennifer L. Knox, Jeremy Gara, Ken Kwapis, Ilya Kaminski, Thomas Sayers Ellis, Katie Jacobs, Ben Foster, Chris Palko, Noelle Kocot, Emily Wells, Harris Hartman, Jillian Roscoe, Alla Plotkin, April Jones, and Keeli Shaw for watering them. Thank you America, Blake, and Alexis for growing with me and letting me grow with you. Thank you Tilda, for the Highlands, where many of these poems were written, and for Sandro, and the gift of giving myself permission to say no. Thank you Neil LaBute, for "phenomena" and everything else misspelled. Jack Hirschman, your name must be in every book I ever write, so here it is.

Thank you Mindy Nettifee, again, because it needs to be said twice.

This book is in memory of Wanda Coleman, for teaching me how to fight, and with what. Diane Di Prima, thank you for yelling, "Amber, just get back on the damn road!" when we were lost that one night on Treasure Island in San Francisco. I needed that.

Brendan Constantine, thank you for the poems "Francis Farmer" and "Quentin Dean."

Christin O'Keefe Aptowicz: This book would not have been finished without your commitment to it and to me. Thank you for fielding my many despairs along the way.

Thank you to all the artists who created for this book: David Lynch, Marcel Dzama, Adrian Tomine, George Herms, Sage Vaughn, Kid Koala, Travis Louie, Sandro Kopp, Pat Hamou, and my papa, Russ. And for you, Manson, whom I can't really thank, I'll thank Lily instead.

Thank you Michael Robbins for editing these poems in their fresh infancy and tirelessly reminding me of the difference between "It's" and "its." You are a friend for life.

Thank you Fred Sasaki, Travis Nichols, Matt Hart and *Forklift Ohio*, Ben Greenberg, Jeff Shotts, Harry Stecopoulos and the *Iowa Review*, Joe

Tiefenthaler, Emily Cole Kelly and the *Paris Review*, and Stephen Elliott and *The Rumpus* for believing in these poems and this book and for reaching out, many, many times, on their behalf.

Matthew Zapruder: Without that first email, and subsequent support, I'm not sure where I'd be. Thank you for sticking your neck out. It is a very fine and sturdy neck.

Thank you Nancy Gates for being a rare bird in a tree of clones. Thank you Anthony Mattero at Foundry Media for representing the shit out of this book. Thanks Alison Granucci and everyone at Blue Flower Arts. Fuck, this is a lot of thank-yous. Okay. Thank you to everyone at Harper Perennial, to Jessica Jarmoune, and to a lady named Linda from the National Archives for aiding in the extensive research of obscure actresses for the list that appears in the Epilogue.

Thank you Calvert Morgan, for knowing exactly what I'm capable of. Without you I would have probably ended up self-publishing this in the form of toilet paper, whiskey, and a nail gun. I guess that also would have made for a good book, but I like the one we made better.

This book is also dedicated to David. What can I write that you don't already know? Thank you for letting me enter into the dark without ever questioning whether I would return. I love you.

## Artwork

Many thanks to the following artists for contributing their work:

Sage Vaughn for Miriam Lebelle (page 6)
Sandro Kopp for Judith Barsi (page 9)
Russ Tamblyn for Peg Entwistle (page 10)
Marcel Dzama for Martha Anne Dae (page 16)
George Herms for Jayne Mansfield (page 18)
Kid Koala for Carol Landis/Anissa Jones (pages 20–21))
Pat Hamou for Jane Doe (page 34)
Marilyn Manson for Sharon Tate (page 45)
Adrian Tomine for Jennifer Davis/Alison Andres (page 50)
Travis Louie for Dana Plato (page 57)
David Lynch for Laurel Gene (page 69)